CYNTHIA RYLANT

Mr. Putter & Tabby
Feed the Fish

Illustrated by

ARTHUR HOWARD

sandpiper

Houghton Mifflin Harcourt

Boston New York

For Robbie, who loves his fish
—C. R.

To Beverly, Earl, and Rachel
—A. H.

Text copyright © 2001 by Cynthia Rylant
Illustrations copyright © 2001 by Arthur Howard

www.hmhco.com

First Harcourt paperback edition 2001

Library of Congress Cataloging-in-Publication Data
Rylant, Cynthia.
Mr. Putter & Tabby feed the fish/Cynthia Rylant;
illustrated by Arthur Howard.
p.   cm.
Summary: After Mr. Putter buys three goldfish and takes them home,
he discovers that his cat Tabby has a serious problem with them.
[1. Cats—Fiction.   2. Goldfish—Fiction.]
I. Title: Mr. Putter and Tabby feed the fish.   II. Howard, Arthur, ill.   III. Title.
PZ7.R982Msd   2001
[E]—dc21   99-50504
ISBN: 978-0-15-202408-6 hardcover
ISBN: 978-0-15-216366-2 paperback

Manufactured in China
SCP   25 24 23 22
4500579903

1

The Fish Store

Mr. Putter and his fine cat, Tabby,
loved going to the fish store.
Mr. Putter loved it because he had owned
goldfish as a boy.
He had always liked goldfish.

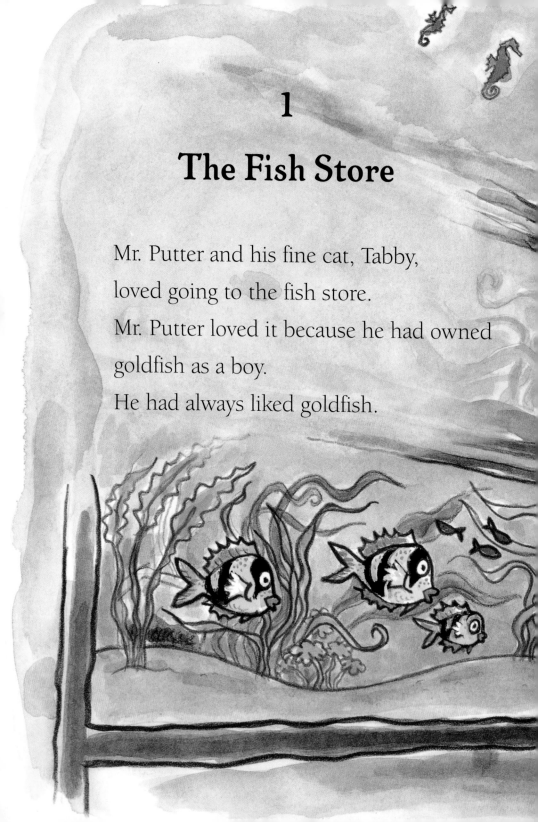

Tabby loved it because it made
her whiskers tingle and
her tail twitch.
Tabby was old, but she still
loved excitement.
And fish were exciting!

One day Mr. Putter and Tabby
were watching the fish in
the fish store when Mr. Putter said,
"Let's bring some home."
It had been many years
since Mr. Putter had owned fish.
He thought it would be fun
to have some again.
It would make him feel
like a boy.

And it would be good exercise
for Tabby's tail.

"We'll take three and a nice big bowl," Mr. Putter said to the fish man.

Mr. Putter and Tabby drove
their fish home.
Tabby nearly twitched herself
right out of the car.
She wasn't sure she could handle
this much excitement!

2

Bat

Back at home, Mr. Putter got the
fishbowl ready.
He dropped the three fish in.

    Plop.

        Plop.

            Plop.

Then he gave them some food.

The fish seemed very happy.

They swam and swam and ate and ate.

Mr. Putter watched.
And Tabby batted.
Bat. Bat. Bat.
"Don't bat the fish, Tabby,"
said Mr. Putter.

But Tabby couldn't help it.

She got all twitchy.

Bat went her paw on the glass.

"No batting," said Mr. Putter.

Bat.

Bat.

Bat. Bat.

Finally Mr. Putter said,

"Come on, Tabby, let's go to bed.

We'll watch the fish tomorrow."

Tabby *wanted* to go to bed.

She *needed* to go to bed.

She was tired from all that batting.

But she couldn't move.

"Bedtime, Tabby," said Mr. Putter.

Bat. Bat. Bat.

Mr. Putter looked at Tabby.

Mr. Putter looked at the fish.

"Hmmm," he said.

He went to get a pillowcase.
He put it over the fishbowl.
"*Now* can we go to bed?"
he asked Tabby.

Tabby purred and followed him to bed.

3

Bat. Bat. Bat.

The next morning when Mr. Putter
woke up, Tabby wasn't there.
"Tabby?" he called.
He listened.

He thought he could hear something.
It sounded very faint.
It sounded very far away.
But he thought he could hear it.
It went: *Bat. Bat. Bat.*

"Oh dear," said Mr. Putter.
He rose from bed and put
on his slippers.
He went downstairs to the fishbowl.

The pillowcase was still over it.
But the pillowcase had grown a tail.

Mr. Putter lifted off the pillowcase.

There was Tabby.

Her eyes were wide.

Her fur was pointy.

Her tail was terribly twitchy.

"Tabby, dear," said Mr. Putter,
"I think you have a fish problem."

Mr. Putter got a bucket.

He put it over the fishbowl.

"Can we have
breakfast now?"
he asked Tabby.

Tabby purred and followed
him to breakfast.

They watched birds instead of
fish while they ate.
Tabby didn't have a bird problem.
Mr. Putter was glad.
He wasn't sure he could get all
those birds under one bucket.

4

So Relaxed

The bucket stayed over the fishbowl
for a week.
Mr. Putter tried taking it off
a few times.
But Tabby got all twitchy and batty
and he had to put it back on.

Finally Mr. Putter got tired of
looking at an upside-down bucket.

"Tabby," he said one morning,
"Let's see if Mrs. Teaberry
would like some fish."

Mrs. Teaberry was Mr. Putter's neighbor.
She usually liked everything.

"*Certainly!*" said Mrs. Teaberry
when Mr. Putter phoned.
"Zeke and I would love some fish!"
(Zeke was Mrs. Teaberry's good dog.)

Mr. Putter and Tabby carried the
fishbowl over.
Mr. Putter told Mrs. Teaberry
about Tabby's fish problem.

Mrs. Teaberry was very nice.

She said that fish make a lot of cats

twitchy and batty.

That made Tabby feel better.

Mr. Putter and Tabby had milk and
cookies with Mrs. Teaberry and Zeke.

Then they said good-bye to the fish
and went home.

Everything was great after that.

It turned out that Zeke did *not*
have a fish problem.
Fish did not make him twitchy.
Fish did not make him batty.

Fish just made him very, very *sleepy*.
Whenever Zeke needed to relax,
he watched his fish.

Zeke was *so* relaxed!

Mr. Putter and Tabby were relaxed, too.
Of course, they had always been very good
at relaxing—except with fish.

They just curled themselves into
Mr. Putter's warm chair and slept.
(Without a single twitch.)

The illustrations in this book were done in in pencil, watercolor,
gouache, and Sennelier pastels on 90-pound vellum paper.
The display type was set in Minya Nouvelle, Agenda, and Artcraft.
The text type was set in Berkeley Old Style Book.
Printed and bound by RR Donnelley,China
Production supervision by Sandra Grebenar and Pascha Gerlinger
Series cover design by Kristine Brogno and Michele Wetherbee
Cover design by Brad Barrett
Designed by Arthur Howard and Carolyn Stafford